Noodle

by April Pulley Sayre

illustrated by Stephen Costanza

Macri

The Pasta Superhero

Orchard Books New York

An Imprint of Scholastic Inc.

Easy

Sayre

Text copyright © 2002 by April Pulley Sayre
Illustrations copyright © 2002 by Stephen Costanza

Library of Congress Cataloging-in-Publication Data
Sayre, April Pulley.
Noodle man : the pasta superhero / by April Pulley Sayre ; illustrated by Stephen Costanza.
p.   cm.
Summary: Al Dente's invention of a portable pasta machine turns him into a superhero
and helps to save the family's fresh-pasta business.
ISBN 0-439-29307-3 (alk. paper)
[1. Pasta products—Fiction. 2. Humorous stories.] I. Costanza, Stephen, ill. II. Title.
PZ7.S2758 No   2001   [E]—dc21   00-66539

10 9 8 7 6 5 4 3 2 1   '02 03 04 05

Printed in Singapore 46
First edition, April 2002

Book design by Mina Greenstein. The text of this book is set in 16 point Tekton.
The illustrations are watercolor.

To my editor, Rebecca Davis, and to Tamson Weston, for keeping my noodles from getting soggy. Thanks also to the pasta pool party—Jeff, Chris, Becky, Patti, Ken, Michael, and Randy—for their brainstorms.—A.P.S.

With love to my parents, Theresa and Joe, who fed me the grapes, vines and all—S.C.

Al Dente was born into a pasta-loving family. His mom and dad ran a fresh-pasta deli. His grandpa invented pasta shapes. His grandma knitted sweaters from spaghetti.

Al tried to be different.
He trained to be a dentist, but
the false teeth he made were
shaped like macaroni.

He went to automotive school, but was kicked out for installing his pasta lunch instead of car parts.

Finally Al joined the family business. The only problem: it was losing money. People in the town of Durum weren't buying fresh pasta anymore. They all wanted pizza delivery. It was so easy.

"We'll have to close the deli," said Papa Dente sadly.

"No, we won't!" said Al. He couldn't bear to fail again.

"Pizza!" announced a delivery person at the door.

"Wrong house!" bellowed Grandpa Dente.

Al watched the pizza delivery person leave. There was something about her. . . .

"Wait, Grandpa. I have an idea!" said Al. He disappeared into the storeroom.

Four days later he emerged with his invention. "It's the world's first adjustable, portable, fresh-pasta maker: any noodle, any shape, any size!"

"We'll put pizza deliverers out of business," said Grandma Dente.

"Fresh ideas. Fresh pasta. That's my son," said Mama Dente.

Al hoisted the contraption onto his back.

"Pasta! Pasta! Fresh pasta!" he called, walking the streets. It was almost dinnertime. Yet no one wanted fresh pasta.

"Bring us a pizza," one guy yelled.

Discouraged, Al started home. Rounding a corner, he saw a frightening sight: three thieves were trying to break into a store.

Al hid. What else could he do, with his little noodle arms? Shaking with fear, he accidentally jiggled a lever.

Chugga, chugga, phloooomp! Angel hair pasta came shooting out of his machine. Springy, stringy, slick, it landed on the crooks.

Terrified, Al ran.

When the police arrived, they were shocked to find the thieves tangled up in sticky pasta.

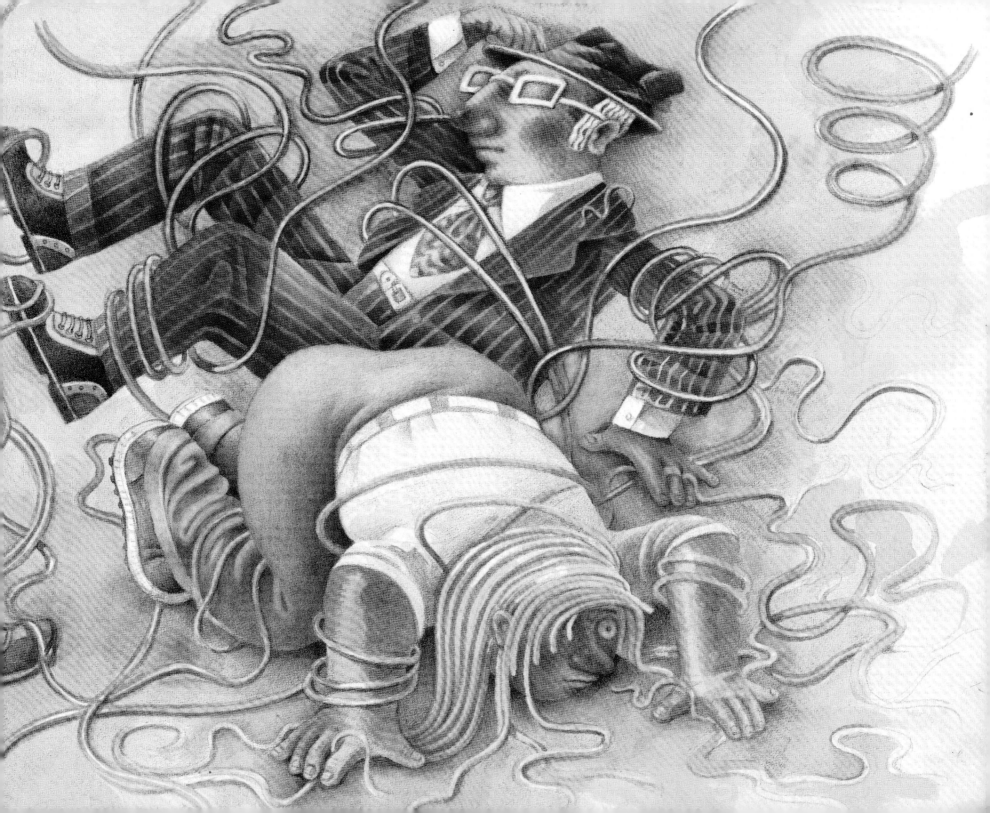

The next night, wearing his farfalle tie, Al headed out
to try pasta delivery again.

"How's the pasta selling?" asked his grandpa.

"Manicotti marvelous!" said Al cheerfully. He didn't
want to disappoint his family.

"Pasta! Pasta! Fresh pasta!" he called, walking the streets. But no one wanted any.

"Who cares!" people said, opening up pizza boxes.

Down near Quadrucci's Al smelled smoke. Suspecting a cookout, he followed the scent. It was a burning building! Two boys were trapped on the second floor!

"Help! Help! Help!" the boys cried. Quickly Al dialed 911.

But what else could he do?

He cranked up his pasta machine.
Chugga, chugga, phloooomp!
A giant lasagna noodle shot up
into the air.

It stuck to the windowsill.
The two boys jumped onto the
noodle and slid down. As they ran
into their parents' arms, Al left.

Firefighters arrived, put out
the fire, and puzzled over
the pasta slide.

"Pasta! Pasta! Fresh pasta!" he called,
walking the streets. No one responded.

He came across a crowd of people
gathered on a curb. A water pipe had broken
and flooded the street. The people couldn't cross.

Hmm . . . thought Al. *How about . . .*

He switched on the machine and turned a dial.

Chugga, chugga, phloooomp!
Out came fusilli—corkscrew pasta. People tied the fusilli to their feet.

Sproing! Sproing! Sproing!
They jumped across the flooded street. Al fusilli-bounced away before anyone could recognize him.

That evening rumors flew about Noodle Man. Who <u>was</u> he?

"He's a superhero!" kids said. They made up games in his honor and even invented new jump-rope rhymes.

"Eenie, meenie, fettucine, linguine.

Ravioli, capelletti, tortellini, ziti, ziti,

Ravioli, capelletti, tortellini, ziti, ziti,

Penne, penne, penne, penne . . . yeah!"

Still, the next day, when they saw Al coming, it never even occurred to them that he was Noodle Man. His suit was in the wash, and he just didn't look like a superhero.

They didn't understand the power of spaghetti-skinny arms.

"Pasta! Pasta! Fresh pasta!" he called, walking the streets. Once again, not a noodle was sold.

Discouraged, Al went home early. His grandpa was waiting in the living room.

"We think you have the right idea, son," Grandpa said. "We decided the delivery business should expand."

In walked Uncle Orzo and cousin Mac Aroni, with two more portable pasta machines.

Al's heart sank like a raw bean in minestrone. How could he tell them that pasta delivery was a failure? He was trying to think of something to say, when . . .

Crash! Crunch! Ka-boom!

The lights dimmed, then died. Al, his family, and everyone else in the neighborhood ran out into the street.

A pizza delivery truck had hit a power pole, bounced off, caught fire, and landed in the town fountain. The driver had been thrown atop the dancing giraffe statue.

"My wrist is sprained. I can't climb down," yelled the pizza truck driver.

The fire was blazing, and the fountain water was heating up!

Al knew what to do. Quick as a slurp of spaghetti, he ran forward.

Chugga, chugga, phloooomp! He shot a sticky linguine noodle over a street lamp. Then he swung up to the statue and landed on the giraffe's back.

Uncle Orzo tried to make fettucine and follow. But . . .

chugga, chugga, blop! All he got was perciatelli, like thin hoses.

"We'll swing off together," Al told the pizza truck driver, a lovely dark-haired woman named Mari Nara.

The flames were reaching higher. The fountain water was boiling. The scene was getting steamy. And the steam was cooking Al's linguine. So when he grabbed the noodle to swing . . . it broke!

"Quick, use your noodle!" Al yelled to Uncle Orzo. Uncle Orzo didn't understand. Grandma Dente did. She grabbed one of the perciatelli, hooked it to a fire hydrant, and turned the hydrant on.

Out shot water, dousing the fire.

"Hurray!" yelled the crowd. But Al and Mari were still in hot water—or at least above it.

Mama Dente grabbed the pasta maker from Mac. After a burst of alphabet pasta—
chugga, chugga, phloooomp!—she shot out two humongous, cheese-filled ravioli.

"Jump!" she yelled to Al.

One, two, three . . . Al and Mari jumped.

Splunsch! Splunsch! They landed on the ravioli, which exploded, squirting cheese. But Al and Mari were safe and sound.

"Noodle Man, hurray! Bravo, Grandma Dente!" the crowd roared.

A reporter stepped up to interview Al.

"So, Noodle Man, what's it like, being a pasta superhero?"

"Well," said Al, "it's really, really . . ."

"Yummy!" shrieked three-year-old Stelline. She had picked a piece of steamed pasta off the fountain edge and was happily nibbling it.

Believe it or not, that was how the residents of Durum rediscovered just how delicious fresh pasta can be. That night, over a bonfire, they cooked up pots of pasta. It was truly a pasta pig-out.

The next day everybody started buying fresh pasta. Al began training community-watch noodle brigades. At night he cooked pasta dinners for Mari at her house. (After all, she couldn't spin pizza dough with her sprained wrist.)

Meanwhile locals and tourists packed the family store. Mama Dente, who's no slouch at business, started packaging pasta in a special way. Sales went through the roof, and almost as fast as pasta boils, the family business was saved!

Noodle Knowledge

Pasta is made of durum wheat mixed with water. This wheat-and-water dough is kneaded. Then it is fed into a machine that squeezes it into ribbons, tubes, sheets, stars, and other shapes. These shapes have many different names in Italian.

To cook pasta properly, put it in boiling water and cook until it is chewable but not mushy. Drain it and add your favorite sauce. Perfectly cooked pasta is slightly firm when you bite it and is said to be "al dente," meaning "to the tooth."

Back home, Al didn't want to tell his family he hadn't sold any pasta. He fed the leftovers to the dog.

His mother was waiting in the kitchen. She had made him a tomato-red suit that said "Noodle Man."

Naturally Al was embarrassed to wear the suit. Yet the next day he wore it anyway, because he loved his mom.